# Hot Stuff

## Written by Margaret Clark
## Illustrated by Tom Jellett

An easy-to-read SOLO
for beginning readers

SOLOS

Southwood Books Limited
3-5 Islington High Street
London N1 9LQ

First published in Australia by Omnibus Books 1998

This edition published in the UK under licence from
Omnibus Books by
Southwood Books Limited, 2002

Text copyright © Margaret Clark 1998
Illustrations copyright © Tom Jellett 1998

Cover design by Lyn Mitchell

ISBN 1 903207 54 1

Printed in Hong Kong

A CIP catalogue record for this book is available
from the British Library

*For Naomi – M.C.*

*For Lucy and Robin – T.J.*

## Chapter 1

When Harry came home from school he saw a van in the driveway. On top of the van was a huge round doughnut shape, big enough for a lion to jump through.

Harry ran inside.
"Hey, Mum, who owns that van?"
he said. "And where is *our* car?"

"Dad sold our car and got the van instead," said Mum. "It has a little kitchen inside it. We can make hot doughnuts there, and sell them. Everyone loves hot doughnuts!"

Harry looked at his mum. "Why would people come to our house to buy doughnuts?" he asked.

"We won't sell them here," said Mum. "We'll drive the van around to all sorts of places. You and Megan can come and help us on the weekends."

"Wow!" said Harry. "I *love* doughnuts!"

When Dad came home they all sat down at the table for tea.

"We need a name for the van," said Dad.

"I know!" said Harry. "It's a van to sell hot doughnuts, right? So let's call it Hot Stuff!"

**Chapter 2**

On Saturday morning Dad backed Hot Stuff out into the street. The van was much bigger than their old car. Bushes on each side of the driveway scratched the paint.

Then Dad backed into a pole.
*Crash!* The back of the van had a
*big* dent in it.

"Wow," said Harry. "Hot Stuff doesn't look so hot now!"

"Never mind," said Mum. "When we've sold lots of hot doughnuts we can buy some paint and fix it all up like new."

## Chapter 3

They drove to the beach, and Dad parked the van on the cliff top.

Harry and Megan looked at all the people in the water and on the sand.

There were families with beach bags and umbrellas.

There were surfers carrying surf-boards and teenagers flicking each other with towels.

There were all sorts of people walking all sorts of dogs.

All along the beach, as far as they could see, there were people having fun.

"I hope they're all hungry," said Harry.

"Let's get cooking," Mum smiled.

## Chapter 4

The yummy smell of hot doughnuts drifted across the beach, and soon there was a long line of people standing in front of Hot Stuff.

"I'll have four jam doughnuts,"
said a lady with three children.

"Six sugar doughnuts for me," said a very fat man.

"Three cinnamon doughnuts, please," said a girl. She took a big bite and burnt her mouth. "Ouch!"

"Watch out," said Harry. "These doughnuts are *hot stuff*!"

Mum, Dad, Harry and Megan worked hard. It was very hot in the van, and by lunchtime they all needed a rest.

"Let's close up the van and go for a walk," said Dad.

"That's the best idea I've heard yet," said Harry.

## Chapter 5

Mum locked the door of the van. "Let's go down to the beach," she said. "Quick, before anyone else asks for a doughnut!"

"I want to have a swim," said Megan.

"You'll sink. You are *full* of jam doughnuts," said Harry.

They were only half way down the steps when they heard a very big BANG.

They all jumped, then turned around and looked behind them. Oh no! Hot Stuff had blown up! This was terrible!

Doughnuts were flying through the air. Everywhere!

"It's raining doughnuts," yelled Harry.

27

Dad and Mum stood there with their mouths open. *Zap! Zap!* Two doughnuts landed in their mouths.

Megan started to giggle. But it wasn't funny. It was a doughnut DISASTER!

## Chapter 6

Harry looked around.

The fat man had a jam doughnut on his bald head.

Beside him was a big black dog with three sugar doughnuts on its tail.

Two cinnamon doughnuts were stuck to a lady's sunglasses.

Lots of flying doughnuts had landed on the beach. A little boy was filling his bucket as fast as he could.

There were four doughnuts on an umbrella spike.

Out on the sea, a surfer found
three doughnuts on the fins of his
surfboard. He looked very surprised!

Someone had rung the fire brigade. In a few moments a fire truck raced up.

A police car came screaming up right behind it, and two policemen jumped out.

It wasn't long before a TV van
arrived with a TV camera man and
a reporter.

"Wow!" said Harry. "We'll be on the news!"

Everyone had come to see the Big Doughnut Disaster!

## Chapter 7

"I think the gas bottle blew up," Dad said to the reporter.

"Just as well you weren't in the van," said one of the policemen.

Harry looked at Mum and Dad and Megan. He was glad they were all still safe.

"Maybe selling hot doughnuts was a bad idea," he said.

"What about Hot Stuff?" asked Megan. She started to cry. "It's in bits and pieces."

Everyone stared at what was left of Hot Stuff.

"Poor Hot Stuff," said Harry.

The fat man who had asked for six sugar doughnuts came over, still munching his last doughnut.

"I *am* sorry about your van," he said. "These are the best doughnuts I've ever tasted."

He gave Dad a card. It said *Big Pete Food Stores*.

"Would you like to make doughnuts for me?" he said. "I will send them all over the country."

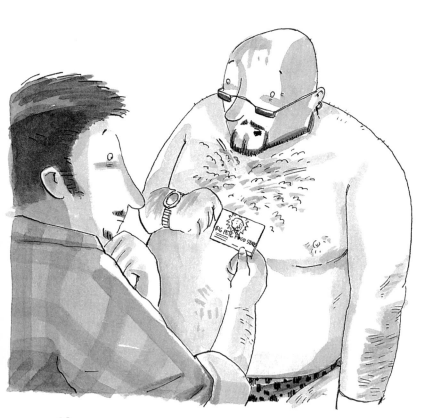

## Chapter 8

So Dad and Mum started making doughnuts for Big Pete.

They made them in their kitchen at home, and after school Megan and Harry helped put them in boxes.

Big Pete had lots of vans to collect the doughnuts, and every van had *Hot Stuff* written on it. It was a *lot* of work making enough doughnuts to fill up all those vans.

44

It wasn't long before Dad said, "I'm getting tired of making doughnuts."

"Our house *smells* like a dough-nut," said Megan.

"There's even sugar in my bed," said Mum.

"I think I'm sick of doughnuts too," said Harry.

When Harry came home from school the next day, there was a red van parked in the driveway. On its side was a sign that said *Noodles on the Move.*

"Wow!" said Harry. "I *love* noodles!"

49

**Margaret Clark**

One day, when I was driving my car, I heard on the news that a doughnut van had blown up in Melbourne. This gave me a great idea for a story, so I pulled over to think about it. I shut my eyes, and I imagined I could see doughnuts flying through the air. They landed on people's heads, on their umbrellas, on their noses, on dogs' tails …

Then I thought: This would be even better if it happened at a beach. Just think of all the places doughnuts could land! And then I went home and wrote the story.

**Tom Jellett**

This story made me think of all the food people eat when they are down at the beach – not only hot doughnuts, but hamburgers, steak sandwiches, fish and chips (I love fish and chips) and lots of lemonade or Coke.

When I'm at the beach I have to buy extra chips, because I always seem to give half of them to a one-legged seagull. (There's always a one-legged seagull on the beach, and I end up feeling sorry for it!)

# More Solos!

## Dog Star
Janeen Brian and Ann James

## The Best Pet
Penny Matthews and Beth Norling

## Fuzz the Famous Fly
Emily Rodda and Tom Jellett

## Cat Chocolate
Kate Darling and Mitch Vane

## Jade McKade
Jane Carroll and Virginia Barrett

## I Want Earrings
Dyan Blacklock and Craig Smith

## What a Mess Fang Fang
Sally Rippin

## Cocky Colin
Richard Tulloch and Stephen Axelsen